TEC

Scrapbooks of America™

Published by Tradition Books® and distributed to the school and library market by The Child's World®

P.O. Box 326, Chanhassen, MN 55317-0326 ➤ 800/599-READ ➤ *http://www.childsworld.com*

Photo Credits: Cover: Rufus F. Folkks/Corbis, (film reel) Royalty-Free/Getty Images, Inc.; Bettmann/Corbis: 10, 12, 13, 15, 18, 21, 22, 24, 25, 28, 34, 35, 40; W.Perry Conway/Corbis: 7; Rufus F. Folkks/Corbis: 16; Craig Lovell/Corbis: 6, 9; Hulton-Deutsch Collection/Corbis: 32; Charles E. Rotkin/Corbis: 30, 38; Brian A. Vikander/Corbis: 39; Getty/Hulton Archive: 11, 17

An Editorial Directions book

Editorial Directions, Inc.: E. Russell Primm, Editorial Director; Lucia Raatma, Line Editor, Photo Selector, and Additional Writing; Katie Marsico, Assistant Editor; Olivia Nellums, Editorial Assistant; Susan Hindman, Copy Editor; Susan Ashley, Proofreader; Alice Flanagan, Photo Researcher and Additional Writer

Design: The Design Lab

Library of Congress Cataloging-in-Publication Data

Dell, Pamela.

  Gavilan : a story of Hollywood during the McCarthy era / by Pamela J. Dell.

    p. cm.—(Scrapbooks of America)

Summary: Seventh grader Ben and his family move to Salinas, California, after Ben's father, a Hollywood actor, is falsely accused of being a communist in 1954 and is blacklisted by the entertainment industry.

  ISBN 1-59187-041-0 (library bound : alk. paper)

  [1. Blacklisting of entertainers—Fiction. 2. United States—History—1953–1961—Fiction. 3. Fathers—Fiction. 4. Moving, Household—Fiction.] I. Title.

PZ7.D3845 Gav 2003

[Fic]—dc21   2003009660

Scrapbooks of America™

GAVILAN

A Story of Hollywood during the McCarthy Era

by Pamela Dell

TRADITION BOOKS®
A New Tradition in Children's Publishing™

MAPLE PLAIN, MINNESOTA

table of contents

"I hate it here!"

I screamed. "How come we have to live here in this stupid place? I want to go back to Hollywood and be with Mom!"

My dad looked at me for a moment, his eyes serious, and maybe, I thought, even sad. But before he had a chance to give me the same old excuse he always did, I ran for the screen door and pushed outside. I ran through the scrubby backyard and bolted out the back gate. I raced down the alley till I came to the dirt road that ran along the end of our block and eventually wound its way to the Salinas River.

I ran hard and I ran fast till I was almost five blocks from home. I didn't want him

6

Salinas seemed like a million miles from Hollywood, and my life had changed so much since we moved there.

I wondered what it would be like to be able to fly— to be free—like a sparrow hawk.

chasing me. If any of the kids in this town saw us, they'd just have more reason to give me trouble. I slowed up and finally stopped to catch my breath in the deep, cool shade of an oak tree. It was a hot Saturday afternoon in early June 1954, and to the east, beyond the little town of Salinas, I could see the Gabilan Mountains in the distance. They rose in pale golden mounds, soft-looking and **serene.** Staring at those mountains gave me a kind of deep stillness inside.

Grandma had told me that the mountains had gotten their name from the Spanish *gavilan,* which meant "sparrow hawk." I said the Spanish word softly under my breath, imagining what it would be like to be a hawk myself. I would rise up into the air on powerful wings. I would sail over those mountains, hover on the **updrafts,** scream out my power, and dive with all the force in my bird body. Then I would **hurtle** upward again and fly away, free of everything that had been dragging me down this past year.

Watching the dark shapes of the real *gavilanes* gliding above the mountains, wings outstretched, made me feel almost like I could forget how bad things were now. But I couldn't really. Things were nothing but a big, fat mess. I kicked at a patch of weeds and started off in the direction of the river, head down and hands in my pockets. But I had gone only a few yards when I heard someone call my name.

"Ben!" she called. "Where are you going?" I turned my head to the left to see my sister, Brady, coming toward me from a side street. Her blond ponytail swung brightly in the sun, and she carried a magazine in her hand. I knew she had been downtown with Carol, her one and only friend in this place. Moving here hadn't been any easier for Brady than it had been for me, so even though she was in eighth grade while I was in seventh, we had been getting along a lot better since leaving Los Angeles. She was the only one who totally understood how I felt.

"River," I said. "You want to come?"

Brady hesitated. "That's kind of far."

"So?" I replied. "Who cares?"

"What happened?" Brady said immediately.

My grandmother lived in Salinas and welcomed us into her home, but I missed the life we had before.

"Dad found out the part in that New York play wasn't coming through either," I told her. "He says his acting days are over and he's just going to stick with his job at the Starlite until he figures out what we should do next."

The Starlite was the drive-in movie theater just outside of town. That was as close as our dad was getting to the movies these days, and it made me sick.

For a minute Brady didn't say anything, and then she grabbed my elbow gently. "Come on," she said. "Let's go back. Maybe we can talk to him."

Even though I considered her suggestion a useless waste of time, I let her persuade me to head back toward home. But we had gone

For many years, drive-in theaters were very popular. People watched movies outside on big screens, usually while sitting in their cars.

Dad was really an actor, but he had to work in a drive-in theater like this one.

Sunset Boulevard in Hollywood,
a glamorous place for sure

only a block when I noticed bully boy Hank Trout sitting on the back of his dad's pickup outside of their house. His mean, narrow eyes watched us as we approached.

"Don't say anything to him," Brady warned in a low voice. We both looked straight ahead, as if we weren't even aware he was there. But just as we came up alongside the truck, he whistled, long and sharp.

"Well, if it ain't the little Hollywood King and Queen," he hooted. "Where's your big actor dad now?"

I clenched my teeth. If I were a hawk, I thought, I would dive-bomb him so fast. I'd tear out all the ugly, greasy hair on the top of his head, pull it out by the roots, and fly off with the whole chunk. I stole a glance at

Hank from the corner of my eye. He had a toothpick stuck in his back teeth and a mean smile plastered on his face.

"I know where he is, that Commie loser," Hank continued, when neither Brady nor I said anything. "He's pushing popcorn in some crusty old drive-in. What a joke!"

With that, I couldn't help myself. I turned and bellowed at Hank, "He's not a Communist! You don't even know what a Communist is, jerk!"

"Shhh!" Brady said instantly, grabbing my arm tight as we hurried on past. "Don't call anyone a jerk, Ben! It's so rude!"

"But he is one, a big dumb one!" I defended. "And look how *he's* talking!"

"Listen, if you let him get to you, it'll

Most people consider Hollywood to be the movie-making captial of the world.

As this newspaper reported, even people like Lucille Ball got caught up in the Communism nonsense.

12

These two screenwriters, Ring Lardner Jr. and Lester Cole, refused to say if they were Communists or not.

just make things all the worse," she advised. "It's like, the minute you talk to him that way, he thinks he's **justified** in being even meaner than he already is."

I hung my head, partly ashamed of myself, but I was still steaming mad.

"We've got to at least *try* to do what's right, just like Dad says," Brady added, "or we'll be lumped in with horrible Hank and everyone like him. We just *can't* let ourselves be like those people."

I knew my sister was right. Beautiful, generous Brady. Proud, wise Brady. If more people acted like she did, I knew, the world would be so much better than it was. But in the ten months we'd lived in Salinas, I had had plenty of time and opportunities to figure out that being generous, proud, and wise took a lot of work. Especially when every day you had to face mean, **judgmental** people who didn't even give you a chance to explain anything. All they did was hate you. Or make fun of you. Without ever really getting to know you.

Before we'd moved, my dad had explained to Brady and me as well as he could what all the trouble in Hollywood was about. He had warned us that it might be hard for a while, living somewhere else and not having as much money as we had in L.A. But before Salinas, I'd never heard anyone speak against my dad even once, especially to my face.

As an actor, Dad hadn't gotten any leading roles yet, but he'd had good parts in big movies, one after another. A lot of people knew his name and his picture had even been in *Photoplay* and other movie magazines. And then suddenly he hadn't been able to get any work at all. The next thing I knew, he, Brady, and I were living in Salinas, California, in an old wood-frame house, with my grandmother and without my mom.

Things were different for my mom. Unlike Dad, she was still getting parts, going on location to shoot movies all over the place. She couldn't stop working, she told us, just because of what had happened to Dad. And, she had added, she couldn't take care of us very well if she was jetting around the world earning the money our dad couldn't

Living in Salinas, I really missed the excitement and glamour of Hollywood.

earn, could she? So of course it would be best for all of us if Brady and I went with Dad, where Grandma could watch over us properly, didn't we both agree? She hugged me then, probably because the shocked look on my face must have annoyed her or something.

"How can you make us leave?!" I'd demanded, still not believing she was really going on her own way without us. Our house in the Hollywood Hills was big and roomy. It had a pool and a maid and lots of extra rooms, including even a **screening room** for watching movies right at home.

At night, on the deck of that house, you could smell the **eucalyptus** as its leaves swished in the warm breezes. You could look

The famous Hollywood sign was constructed in 1922. Each letter is 45 feet (14 m) tall.

The Hollywood sign was huge and could be seen for miles!

16

I missed living in our nice house and swimming in the pool.

down on the city of L.A. and see the glittering, sparkling sprawl of the movie kingdom, with miles and miles of lights heading out toward the darkness of desert. I wanted to keep the life we had there. But suddenly it was all over, because of something called the blacklist.

Dad had tried to explain that, too. The blacklist, he told us, was a secret list of movie business people who were supposedly against the government. People who really supported the Soviet Union and communism, instead of democracy. But he said most of the people on the list had ended up there mainly just because of what other people had said about them. Rumors, lies, and false accusations could land you on the blacklist

These actors, led by Lauren Bacall and Humphrey Bogart, opposed the backlist.

at any time, with no warning. And with no real proof at all. After that, no movie studio would hire you for anything either. Even though, according to Dad, very few on the list were really guilty of anything.

I didn't understand it completely, but I hated the blacklist. Because of it, hundreds of actors and writers and movie directors were suddenly out of work. People were losing their jobs, having to move away, getting divorced—all things that had happened to my dad.

"But they're still making movies!" I had said to him back then, trying to figure it out. He and I were sitting in his study a few weeks before we'd had to give up our house and move. Beyond the window, I could see the patio and the pool, a long inviting stretch of blue, with the sun glistening on the water. But I felt too sick and confused to want to lie on a float with a glass of lemonade in my hand, the way I usually did in the afternoon.

"It's crazy, Ben," my dad had replied, looking up from the newspaper he'd been reading. "This country's in an **uproar** of fear, and fear always makes people do shameful things."

"But what are they afraid of?" I wanted to know.

"You name it. They're afraid someone foreign, or 'Communist,' is going to take their jobs."

"Is it true?"

"Of course it's not true, Ben. Those being

accused are mostly just people with a different point of view on things. Which happens to be one of the basic rights we have in this country—to disagree and object." My dad's voice was calm and serious, but anybody could tell he was pretty upset. "This kind of hysterical thinking is dangerous," he added.

"Why dangerous?" I kept pressing, trying to figure it all out.

"Well, because the hatred and fear it's generating is turning everybody against each other," Dad replied. He folded his newspaper and looked down at it again. "Ordinary citizens are becoming self-appointed watchdogs, out to destroy anyone who seems even faintly suspicious. And this crackpot McCarthy is leading the whole pack now."

Dad's fingers flicked against a photograph on the front page, and I leaned over to look. The image was of a man with thick, dark eyebrows and a mean-looking, wide-open mouth. His front teeth looked like a horrible little row of corn kernels, with big gashes of space between them. The man did seem sort of like a mad dog to me, and if my dad was right, then everything that was happening to us was because of him. His picture made me feel sick. But still, I couldn't stop asking questions, and Dad did his best to answer them all.

He explained how everything had started with a government group called the House Un-American Activities Committee. The committee had begun questioning people they felt were suspicious and had sentenced ten

The House Un-American Activities Committee (HUAC) was originally formed in 1930. The committee set out to prove that the Screen Writers Guild (the people who wrote movie scripts) had Communist members.

This group of Hollywood writers and producers had to appear before McCarthy's committee. Some went to jail for refusing to answer the committee's questions.

Senator *Joseph McCarthy* during one
of the *HUAC* hearings

*People all over the United States
watched the hearings on television.*

men, known as the Hollywood Ten, to jail for being Communists. A few years later, this Joseph McCarthy, a senator from Wisconsin, had started on his own mission to find Communist spies in the government.

"McCarthy's really fueling this whole mess," Dad told me. "He claims there are spies everywhere. In the military, the government, next door to you and me—"

"But there were some," I said, remembering hearing something about it.

"Yes, there have been some real spies caught in the last few years," Dad agreed. "But this McCarthy, despite his unending stream of wild accusations, seems unable to provide anyone with a real list of names, or any proof at all."

"But if he doesn't have any proof, why is anyone even listening to him?" I said.

"That's the mystery, Ben," Dad said, shaking his head. "The sad fact is that, with the right words, people can be easily riled up into a state of hysteria. Who knows why? They react without thinking. They decide something's true without even taking the time to check the facts. And because of that, a lot of innocent lives are being ruined all over Hollywood and the rest of the country, too."

~

As Brady and I got safely past Hank Trout and walked the few final blocks back to the house, I thought about Dad's words. My life had definitely been ruined.

"Let's not go home," I said to Brady

suddenly. "Let's hide in one of those freight train cars and go wherever it takes us! Or maybe we can find one going to L.A. We can go be with Mom."

Brady looked at me a minute as if I were joking. Then she surprised me.

"Okay," she said.

Her agreement gave me energy. "Come on then!" I shouted.

"Only we can't go this minute, Ben. We have to plan it first. We need clothes. And money. And maybe even a schedule for trains to southern California. I don't want to go anywhere else but L.A."

Everything Brady said made sense, and right away a plan started forming in my mind. We would take one knapsack full of clothes

After being blacklisted, some of the Hollywood Ten who were writers used false names in order to continue working in the movie business. Robert Rich, who won an Academy Award for writing *The Brave One* in 1956, was actually Dalton Trumbo, a member of the Hollywood Ten.

Movie star Gary Cooper told *HUAC* that he had turned down some scripts because they contained Communist ideas.

Baseball great Jackie Robinson testified before HUAC and answered questions about Communism and black Americans.

and a second one full of food. And we'd bring all the money we had.

Thoughts of anger and anticipation were swirling in my head as we came up the front steps of the house together. Grandma was sitting on the wide front porch, in her rocker there, shelling peas.

"Where'd you get off to, Benjamin?" she asked me. "Your daddy's worried sick. He's out looking for you still."

"He's a Communist!" I hurled the word out into the air with as much negative force as I could manage. Brady glanced at me with that warning look of hers. We both knew that because of that word my grandmother had lost some of her friends, just for taking us all in. But we weren't spies. We hadn't done anything against the government. We were the same people we'd always been. But right then it felt good, even if in a bad way, to say the harshest thing I could think of.

"Now you listen to me, young man," Grandma snapped, leaning forward to hold me in that fierce stare of hers. "Your daddy is a good man. He stands up for what's right. And if people want to call him a Communist for trying to help poor folks, or for believing we should all—black as well as white, women right along with men—get equal rights, then let 'em think so, and be darned!"

She rocked back in her chair and started shelling her peas again, her hands moving in a furious fashion. Without saying anything, Brady sat down across from her and began to help. Beyond our street, the sun was setting, sending up streaks of purple and orange into the western sky. I settled on the steps, hoping to spot the hawks again, but I could see none from there.

"People around here think you're a Communist if you put your shoes on backwards!" Gram muttered, when neither of us responded to her outburst. "But if they consider themselves true Americans, they'd better darn well remember the First Amendment to our Constitution. Not to mention the Fifth!"

"I know what that is," Brady volunteered. "The Fifth Amendment means a person doesn't have to say things against himself on the witness stand in court."

"That's about right," Gram agreed.

I was still feeling a little edgy. "So, if Dad got accused of being a Communist, he wouldn't be forced to admit it, even if he was?"

"Hmmph!" Gram snorted. "Go ahead and be as clever as you like, Benjamin, but that is exactly how it *should* work."

She dumped a handful of peas into a glass bowl and continued. "We're all supposed to be considered innocent until we're proven guilty beyond a reasonable doubt. But these days, all someone has to do is make a claim against you. If you refuse to say whether or not that claim is true, you might very well land behind bars, and quick! I don't call that American in the slightest."

I listened without saying anything.

"And as for the First Amendment, that guarantees our freedom of speech," she went on. "You got the right to speak your mind about things, even if you disagree with everybody else. That's a legal right, too, and some folks better wake up and realize it. When they start taking that away—especially without going through any legal process at all, as they're managing to get away with every day now—you know you're in a load of trouble."

Just then I heard footsteps moving through the house, and my dad came out on the porch. He looked at me and right away I felt really bad. I didn't need Grandma to tell me how hard he'd been working to take care of us after Mom decided to leave. I knew he was against racism. I knew he'd practically gone

Journalist Edward R. Murrow spoke out against Senator McCarthy and HUAC. He played an important part in ending the committee's work.

On his television show, See it Now, Edward R. Murrow attacked Senator McCarthy and the actions of HUAC.

to jail when he was eighteen for being part of the big Salinas lettuce strike of 1936. All he'd wanted to do then was to help the starving farm workers get a few cents more an hour, before their rich, farm-owning bosses and the military had joined forces to smash down any hopes they'd ever had of that.

When Dad had told me about all the terrible things that had happened back then, I remembered it had seemed as cruel and unfair to me as it had to him. He'd seen the whole thing and tried to do something about it. Grandma was right about him, I realized now, and suddenly I hoped I'd be able to find the strength inside myself to stand up as strong as he always did. But still, I didn't want to have to do it in Salinas.

"I've been hunting you up and down every alley back there, Ben," Dad said. "I'm glad you're home."

I nodded without saying anything. He squeezed my shoulder as he sat down on the steps beside me.

While Dad, Brady, and Gram continued to talk, I found my mind drifting to other things. Things like getting on that train and what it would be like to show up on the doorstep at my mom's new house. I figured when she saw us, she'd be so relieved to have us back that she wouldn't even care if all her crying ruined her eye makeup. In my mind, I realized, I'd already said, *Good-bye, Salinas,* and *So long for now, Dad.*

❦

Brady had somehow found out that a freight train left Salinas every Saturday night at 9:20 for Los Angeles, so that next Saturday we were ready. As soon as Dad had left for the Starlite and Gram had gone down the street to play cards with her friends, we took off.

It seemed even easier than I'd imagined. In the soft air of late spring and dressed in dark clothing, we were like two sly black cats. We slipped down the sidewalks, darted across dark streets, hid behind bushes or trees if we heard footsteps coming.

The moon was just rising above the ghostly outline of the Gabilans as we reached the far edge of the train yard. It hung like a slim silver sword, barely shedding any light on our path. I

Members of the Hollywood Ten, refused to answer the committee's questions, based on their Fifth Amendment rights. But they were put in jail anyway.

Brady and I headed to the train yard, hoping to hitch a ride out of Salinas.

followed Brady through the night as if she were my guardian angel. She claimed to know which train it was that we had to get on, and she always did her homework right. I trusted that she had it right this time, too.

But we were still far from the hub of the yard when, without warning, a flurry of hoarse hissing sounds seemed to surround us. From out of nowhere, four blinding flashlight beams shattered us with light, and we found ourselves encircled by four bulky figures. Their stale smell so close made my stomach reel.

"So, the Hollywood traitor family's out for a stroll!" one of them said. The others laughed, but they didn't sound like they were in a very good mood. The next second, they had pulled our arms behind our backs and were marching us toward the gaping opening of a nearby boxcar.

"Get in! And don't say a word, or else!" someone commanded, shoving me hard. I climbed in behind Brady and then someone ordered us to sit down on the floor. As we did, the four dark shapes sat, too, in a semi-circle in front of us. Their flashlights danced wickedly across our faces. I put my hand up to my brow to shade my eyes from the glare and squinted, letting my gaze sweep past each one. It was a sight worse than any I'd seen in a long time. It was Hank Trout and three of his friends. We were trapped.

Hank spoke first, his voice full of a sneer in the dark. "What do you traitors think

Instead of being on a train headed back to Los Angeles,
we soon found ourselves trapped in a train car.

you're doing out here on our turf, huh?" I opened my mouth to speak, but before a single word came out, Brady's clear voice rose beside me.

"None of your business," she said. I held my breath.

"Ha! You hear that?" one of them snorted. As he looked to the others, I stole a glance at my sister. Her eyes looked fierce and angry rather than afraid, and seeing that gave me courage, too.

"You!" snarled the third boy. He leaned forward and jabbed his flashlight into my chest. "Answer! What are you doing sneaking into our camp, spying?"

"I don't have to answer anything," I said, as calmly as I could.

"Oh yeah?" he replied. "Who says?"

"The Fifth Amendment says," I answered, thinking of what Gram had told us.

"The fifth what?" Hank sneered. "You'll answer, all right."

The fourth boy had been rummaging through our knapsacks, throwing our clothes out onto the dusty floor of the car. Now he looked up and spoke for the first time.

"It's that Commie talk," he said. He took an apple and bit into it, then passed the sack around to the others. "That's the answer all the spies are taught to give."

"Are you or are you not spies for the Russians?" Hank Trout instantly demanded, his mouth stuffed with the brownies we had brought.

"Oh yeah, right!" I replied. My heart felt like it was being squeezed in Hank's fat fist, but I refused to let it show.

"Answer," Hank commanded, "if you don't want to get walloped by this thing!" He held his flashlight threateningly above my head.

Then Brady surprised me again.

"We're Americans!" she cried. "A lot more American than you are, Hank Trout! So we don't have to answer you, and we don't have to agree with anything you think!"

"Yeah!" I shouted. It suddenly seemed as if Brady and I were plugged into the exact same energy source. "And we have a right to say what we think, too, without being attacked! So you'd better let us go, you hear me? Or you'll be sorry!"

The Crucible, a play by Arthur Miller, opened on Broadway in 1953. It tells the story of a witch hunt, a symbol of the unfair practices of HUAC.

These demonstrators opposed the ruling against the Hollywood Ten. I hoped Brady and I could show the same courage they did.

Seven members of the Hollywood Ten signing a document near a statue of Abraham Lincoln in Washington, D.C.; even when put on trial, these men held on to their beliefs.

A sudden rush of electricity came flying through my legs and it brought me right to my feet. Then Brady was up, too. Together, as if a gun had gone off to start a race, we lunged for the doorway of the freight car. But there was no chance. Instantly all four boys were towering over us, blocking our way.

The next few minutes seemed to me like a terrible shadow dance between the forces of dark and light. In the dirty cell of the boxcar, our six shadows loomed and **wavered** against the walls, monstrous in the beams of the flashlights. The noise rose up like a chorus from the underworld. There were grunts and shouts. Screams and hissing. Name calling and hair pulling. Scratches and punches. Thuds and scrapes and the sound of ripping cloth.

And then a grown man's voice boomed out above all of it, powerful and commanding.

"All right, you kids! Every one of you! Get down out of there!" It was the voice of my dad.

There was a hard thump as he jumped up into the car, and I could see his form outlined in the doorway. He grabbed Hank and another boy by their collars, making them look so much smaller now and helpless in his grasp. They both struggled, but my dad had a physical edge on them and they couldn't get away. Then another man hopped into the car. It was a policeman, one I'd seen Dad talking to in town a few times before. Someone I remembered he'd mentioned as being a fair and deep-thinking man.

In the sudden shocked silence, we all came to a standstill. A moment later, the cop was leading Hank and his buddies off toward his squad car. Without too many words, Brady and I tried our best to gather up our scattered belongings, and then we followed Dad to our own car. We sat in silence as Dad drove through the dark streets back toward Gram's house, the headlights marking off the blocks as we went. As we rounded the corner, the house—our home now—came into view. Seeing the cheery lights in the windows there, I felt a lot better than I thought I'd feel.

❧

Brady had a scratch on her cheek and bruises on both arms. I had a black eye, a torn shirt, and a stiff feeling in my knee. But other than that, we were unharmed. Unharmed and grateful that Dad had come to look for us and hadn't given up until he'd found us. It turned out that when Gram had returned home from cards and discovered us missing, she'd called him at work.

After our fight with Hank Trout's gang, Dad confessed to Brady and me that, in order to keep on working, Mom had given names of people she knew to the House Un-American Activities Committee. People who were supposedly Communists.

"She did what she believed was right," he said. "And I don't fault her for that. But that wasn't my way to handle things. So we had to call it quits." He also told us that if we really wanted to go back to her and she agreed, he'd support us fully. But somehow, the more I

understood about everything that had been going on, the less I felt like returning to Hollywood. I wanted to be where Dad was, wherever that was, and so did Brady.

On June 9, just about a week after the train yard episode, Dad and Gram settled in as usual to watch what they called the Army-McCarthy hearings on television. The hearings had been going on practically every day for weeks, and they had to do with Senator McCarthy's claims of spies in the military. This time Brady and I watched, too, as McCarthy seemed to go crazy before our eyes.

"He's scary," said Brady as the hearing seemed to be ending.

"He sure is," Dad agreed. "And he's just given the American public a good look at how destructive he is. I don't think he's going to be around much longer. Maybe this insanity is finally coming to its end." With that Dad switched off the TV and looked around at all of us. I hoped he was right.

"I think we all ought to think about moving to Monterey," he said. "Or maybe Carmel. Maybe I could start a theater company there."

Hearing that, Brady shot me a big grin and I grinned back.

Later that afternoon, I took a long walk, out toward the foothills of the Gabilan Mountains. Above my head, a lone hawk was **soaring** free, and this time I could almost

The McCarthy hearings lasted 36 days and were broadcast on television for 188 hours. Twenty-five million Americans watched the hearings on television.

Monterey was a beautiful place. Thinking about moving there gave me lots of hope for our future.

The gavilanes knew about having a free spirit.
I was beginning to feel that freedom again, too.

Sparrow hawks, *gavilanes,* are small, only about 10 inches (25 centimeters) long. They are usually found flying in wide-open spaces.

feel it was really me up there. The idea of moving to Monterey, and being near the ocean again, was like a dream come true for me.

But freedom, I'd discovered, wasn't about where you lived. It was more about how you lived. It was a big soaring space inside your head that gave you the strength to do the right thing even when it was scary. It was a deep, quiet feeling in your heart that made you want to try to understand other people instead of just going crazy on them if they disagreed with you. And most of all, freedom was about people who loved you, even if they didn't always approve of what you believed or how you behaved. People who loved you, no matter what.

THE HISTORY OF HOLLYWOOD
DURING THE McCARTHY ERA

In the mid-1950s, anti-communist hysteria spread throughout the United States. It was fed by fear that communists had infiltrated American society and were plotting to overthrow the government. Wild rumors and accusations, known as McCarthyism, led to intensive investigations by the U.S. Senate to root out communist spies and eliminate them in the government, the military, the media, and the entertainment industry.

Joseph McCarthy, a Wisconsin senator and chairman of the Government Committee on Operations in the Senate conducted many investigations. Early investigations by the House Un-American Activities Committee targeted the motion picture industry in Hollywood, California. Hundreds of people suspected of "unpatriotic" views were brought before the committee and interviewed. Even though a majority of them were falsely accused, they were blacklisted (refused jobs) and denied their civil rights. Even children of actors, like Ben and Brady, were discriminated against.

McCarthyism developed after World War II as a result of mistrust between communist and capitalist nations. The mistrust, which is still present today, grew out of political differences and the fear that communism would one day replace capitalism in the freedom-loving nations of the world. Communists believe that property should be owned in common and controlled by the government. Capitalists believe that property should be privately owned and controlled by individuals in competition with one another.

Russia, a communist country, contributed to the mistrust that non-communist nations felt after the war. Under the guise of helping war-torn countries recover, Russian troops not only continued to control the countries it occupied but also enforced communism there. The United States believed that Russia intended to spread communism worldwide.

McCarthyism gradually declined after 1954 when televised senate investigations exposed Joseph McCarthy's behavior and the government's failure to protect citizens' freedoms. Today, the term McCarthyism is sometimes used to describe activity that recklessly accuses people of un-American behavior or disloyalty to the United States.

accusations statements, which may or may not be true, of another's wrongdoing

Communist a member of the Communist Party, a government system in which goods are owned by everyone and are available to anyone in need

confessed admitted a mistake

crackpot someone who has crazy ideas and acts in an uncontrolled manner

democracy a government system in which leaders are elected by the people

eucalyptus a sweet-smelling tree that grows in dry climates

Fifth Amendment a change to the Constitution stating that no person has to testify against himself in court

First Amendment a change to the Constitution stating that all people have the right to voice their own opinions

guardian angel someone who protects and looks out for another

hub the center of activity

hurtle to move at a great speed

T I M E L I N E

1908 Joseph McCarthy is born on November 14 in Grand Chute, Wisconsin.

1939–1945 World War II takes place. Though the Soviet Union is an ally of the United States, relations between the governments are strained.

1946 Joseph McCarthy is elected to Congress as a senator from Wisconsin.

1947 The House Un-American Activities Committee was formed in the 1930s, but the first Hollywood investigations and hearings are in 1947. The Hollywood Ten are sentenced to jail and blacklisted.

1950 Senator Joseph McCarthy gives speeches condemning communism. He claims to have a list of known Communists working for the U.S. government.

hysterical uncontrolled and easily excited

judgmental having harsh opinions about something or someone

justified having a good reason for doing something

outburst a sudden outpouring of emotion or speech

riled up annoyed and angry

screening room a room set aside for watching films

serene peaceful and calm

soaring flying high in the air

sprawl an area of land that stretches out from another

updrafts upward movements of air

uproar noise and confusion

watchdogs people who guard against illegal acts

wavered swayed unsteadily

1951 A number of well-known Hollywood writers and actors are called before HUAC, including Orson Welles, Humphrey Bogart, Lucille Ball, Dashiell Hammett, and Lillian Hellman.

1952 Joseph McCarthy is re-elected to the U.S. Senate.

1953 Arthur Miller's *The Crucible* opens at the Martin Beck Theater in New York City.

1954 McCarthy accuses the U.S. Army of having Communists in its ranks. The American public begins to doubt his accusations. In December, the Senate censures McCarthy, criticizing his conduct.

1957 Joseph McCarthy dies on May 2 at the age of forty-nine.

ACTIVITIES

Continuing the Story *(Writing Creatively)*

Continue Ben's story. Elaborate on an event from his scrapbook or add your own entries to the beginning or end of his journal. You might write about his experiences as the son of Hollywood actors or his response to being discriminated against. You can also write your own short story of historical fiction about McCarthyism in Hollywood in the 1950s and its affect on American life.

Celebrating Your Heritage *(Discovering Family History)*

Research your family history. Record the names of relatives who were living in America in the 1950s during the McCarthy Era. How were they involved directly or indirectly in the events? Ask family members to write down what they know about the people and events of this time period. What were their opinions about what happened?

Documenting History *(Exploring Community History)*

Find out how your city or town was affected by the McCarthy Era. Visit your library, a historical society, a museum, or related Web sites for links to important people and events. What did newspapers report at the time? When, where, why, and how did your community respond? Who was involved? What was the result?

Preserving Memories *(Crafting)*

Make a scrapbook about family life in America during the 1950s, or a scrapbook about an actor's life during the McCarthy Era. Imagine what life was like for you or for them. Fill the pages with special events, stories, interviews with relatives, and letters. Include copies of newspaper clippings, postcards, posters, movie magazines, and references to communism. Decorate the pages and cover with pictures of keepsakes, famous actors, local theaters and billboards, and lists of favorite movies and television shows.

TO FIND OUT MORE

At the Library

Finkelstein, Norman H. *With Heroic Truth: The Life of Edward R. Murrow.*
New York: Houghton Mifflin, 1997.

Ritchie, Nigel. *Communism.* Austin: Raintree/Steck-Vaughn, 2002.

Sherrow, Victoria. *Joseph McCarthy and the Cold War.* San Diego: Blackbirch, 1998.

Stein, R. Conrad. *The Great Red Scare.* Glenview, Ill.: Silver Burdett, 1998.

Zeinert, Karen. *McCarthy and the Fear of Communism.*
Berkeley Heights, N.J.: Enslow, 1998.

On the Internet

Censure of Senator Joseph McCarthy
http://usinfo.state.gov/usa/infousa/facts/democrac/60.htm
To read the actual censure of Joseph McCarthy by the Senate

HUAC and Censorship Changes
http://www.moderntimes.com/palace/huac.htm
For more information about HUAC and its effects on Hollywood

HUAC, McCarthy, and the Reds
http://huac.tripod.com
To learn more about the activities of HUAC and the blacklist

Joseph McCarthy
http://www.apl.org/history/mccarthy/
For information about the senator's life

Joseph McCarthy: A Modern Tragedy
http://www.foxvalleyhistory.org/mccarthy/menu.htm
For a look at McCarthy and his effects on American history

Places to Visit

Hollywood Entertainment Museum
7021 Hollywood Boulevard
Hollywood, CA 90028
323/465-7900
To learn more about Hollywood's history

The Outagamie County Historical Society
330 East College Avenue
Appleton, WI 54911
920/733-8445
For more information about McCarthy and his life

Saint Mary's Cemetery
312 South State Street
Appleton, WI 54911
920/739-5119
To see Senator McCarthy's grave